Picture Book of Classical Chinese Tales

中国传统故事美绘本（中英文双语版）

The River Snail Maiden

从前，有个小伙子叫谢端，靠给地主种田为生。他非常勤劳能干，每天天刚亮就起床耕作，太阳下山才回家，种的粮食比别人种的都好。

　　他为人十分忠厚老实，说谎骗人的事从来不做。邻居们有什么事他都乐于帮忙，从不求回报。村里人都很喜欢他。只是因为家里太穷，一直没钱娶妻。

　　A long time ago, a young man named Xie Duan earned his living by doing the farming for the landlord. He was a hardworking man who was busy farming from dawn to dusk and always managed to gather in a better harvest than others.

　　Meanwhile, Xie Duan was such an honest man that he never cheated others and so kind-hearted that he never sought for rewards for his kindness. So the villagers nearby liked him very much, but no one would marry their daughter to him as he was too poor to afford the wedding.

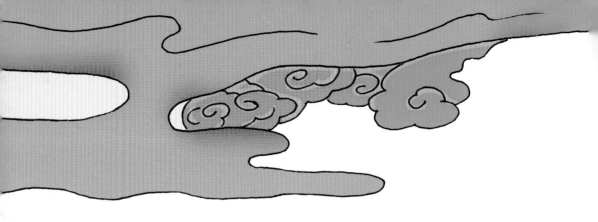

一天，他到田里干活。远远看见有东西闪闪发光。走近一看，原来是一只田螺。这只田螺不仅特别大，而且闪着一种美丽的光泽。小伙子从没见过这么大、这么好看的田螺。他很惊奇，也很喜欢，就把它捧在手里带回家，放在水缸里，精心地养着。

One day while doing the farming, Xie Duan came across something glittering on the ground. It turned out to be a river snail. Xie Duan was pleasantly surprised since he had never seen such a big and shining river snail before, so he took it home and took great care of it in a water tank.

有一天，小伙子一早起来就像往常一样去地里劳动。晚上回到家却被眼前的景象惊呆了。

　　只见桌上放着香喷喷的米饭、美味可口的鱼肉蔬菜，茶壶里烧开的水还冒着热气。他想，咦，家里明明没有人呀？一定是哪位好心的邻居来过帮我做饭了吧？

　　没想到，第二天回到家又是这样。接下来，第三天，第四天……天天如此。

The life went on as usual. But one day when Xie Duan finished his farming to return home, he was taken aback by what he saw. On the table savory rice, delicious food and a steaming kettle of hot water were waiting for him! He decided that, since no one else stayed in his house in the daytime, it must have been one of his nice neighbors who came to help.

But strangely enough, the same weird thing continued to happen every day.

到底是哪位好心人在帮助自己呢？这样可真过意不去。小伙子这样想着，就挨家挨户地到邻居家去道谢。

走了一家又一家，邻居们都说不是自己做的。有的还笑着说："是你自己偷偷娶了个媳妇，帮你烧火做饭吧？"说得他摸不着头脑。回到家里他越想越纳闷，就下决心一定要探个究竟。

"Who is so nice to me? I must go to say thanks," Xie Duan said to himself one day. And then he went from door to door to his neighbors to express his gratitude.

However, none of his neighbors admitted to helping. Some of them even teased Xie Duan, "You must have married a girl in secret, and she does the cooking for you every day, right? " Xie Duan felt even more confused and made up his mind to find out the truth.

于是早上鸡叫头遍,他就像往常一样,扛着锄头下田去劳动。天一亮他就匆匆赶回家,想看一看到底是哪位好心人在帮助他。大老远他就看到自家屋顶的烟囱冒着炊烟,于是加快脚步向家走去。

当他蹑手蹑脚地贴近门缝往里看时,竟发现家里静悄悄的,一个人影也没有。他走进门,却只见桌上饭菜飘香,灶中火仍在烧着,水在锅里沸腾,还没来得及舀起。只是热心的烧饭人不见了。

The next day, Xie Duan went with his hoe before daybreak to do the farming and then rushed home just at dawn. He wanted to find out who was helping him. Far away from his house, Xie Duan could already see the smoke from his kitchen chimney. He quickened his pace.

When he tiptoed to the door and peeped through the crack, he saw no one. He entered and found that the table was already set full of delicacies, the fire was still burning in the stove and the wok was boiling away. Only the cook was nowhere to be found.

第二天早上，小伙子起得更早了，鸡叫头遍就下地干活，天没亮就往家赶。远远地见家里的炊烟还未升起。

他悄悄靠近篱笆，躲在暗处，全神贯注地看着屋里的一切。只见一个年轻美丽的姑娘从水缸里缓缓走出来，奇怪的是身上的衣裳却一点儿也没有湿。这姑娘走到灶前，就开始烧火煮饭做菜。

On the next morning, Xie Duan got up and began his farming even earlier and hurried home before daybreak. This time, the smoke had not yet begun to spiral up from the kitchen chimney.

Xie Duan approached the wattle stealthily and hid himself there to watch what was going on in his house. Suddenly, a pretty girl crept slowly out of the water tank, but strangely, her dress was not damp at all. The girl came to the stove to start the cooking.

小伙子连忙飞快地跑进门，走到水缸边，一看，自己捡回的大田螺只剩下个空壳。他惊奇地拿着空壳看了又看，然后走到灶前，对年轻姑娘说道："请问这位姑娘，你从什么地方来？为什么要帮我做饭？"

姑娘没想到他会在这个时候出现，大吃一惊，听到他盘问自己的来历，不知如何回答，便转身想回到水缸中。小伙子挡住去路，一再追问。姑娘没有办法，只好实话实说，把事情的原委告诉了他。

Xie Duan rushed into his house, hurried to the water tank and looked into it; there he found only the empty shell of the river snail. Picking up the shell, he gazed at it in surprise and then approached the girl. "Excuse me, where are you from? Why do you help me with the cooking?"

The girl, startled to find that Xie Duan should come back home at this time and having no idea how to answer his questions, turned around to go back into the vat. Xie Duan stood in her way and kept repeating his questions. The girl had no choice but to tell him the whole story.

原来，这位姑娘是天上的神女。天帝知道谢端从小失去了父母，一个人孤单地生活，很同情他。又见他为人忠厚，乐于助人，勤劳能干，生活节俭，就很欣赏他，所以派神女下凡帮助他。

The girl turned out to be a fairy maiden. Knowing that Xie Duan had lost his parents as a child and had been leading a lonely life, the God of Heaven had felt deep sympathy for him. And considering that Xie Duan was such an honest, hard-working and frugal man, the God of Heaven decided to send a fairy maiden to help him.

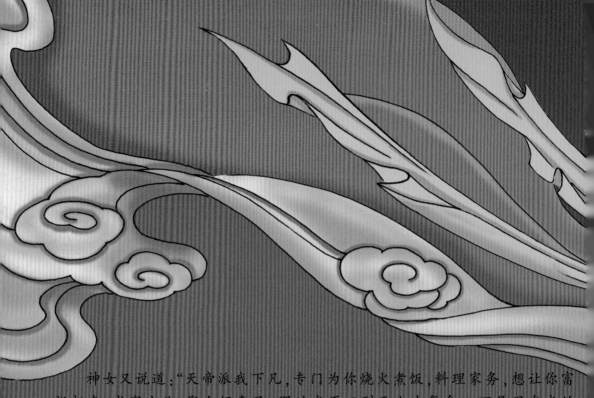

神女又说道："天帝派我下凡，专门为你烧火煮饭，料理家务，想让你富裕起来，成家立业，娶个好妻子，那时我再回到天上去复命。可是现在我的使命还没完成，却被你知道了天机，我的身份已经暴露了。就算你保证不说出去，也难免会被别人知道。我不能再待在这里了，我必须回到天庭去。"

小伙子听完姑娘的一番话，心情十分复杂。既有感激之情，又后悔不该窥破天机。他再三盛情挽留："姑娘，我求你留下来吧。"可是姑娘去意已决。

"The God of Heaven sent me here to do the cooking and other housework for you. I wanted to help you lead a wealthy life. Several years hence, you would have married and settled down. Then I would have gone back to the Heavenly Palace. Now I have given myself away and you know the secret before I have completed the task. Even if you promised me you wouldn't tell others, the truth would soon come out. I can't stay here any longer; I must return to the Heavenly Palace," the fairy maiden told Xie Duan.

Hearing her words, Xie Duan had mixed feelings—grateful for her help and regretful at having insisted on knowing the truth. He repeatedly asked the girl to stay, saying, "Just stay here, please." But it didn't work.

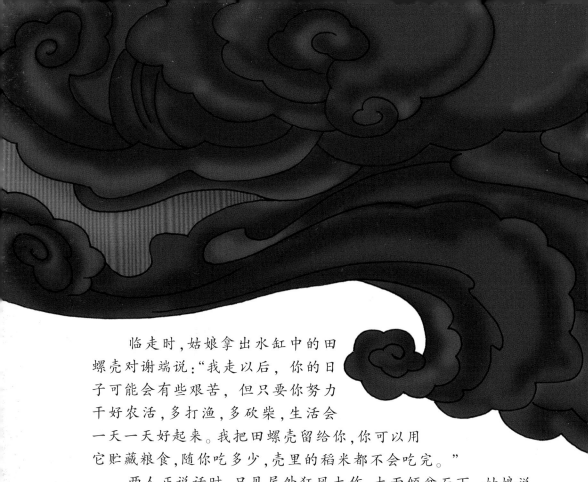

　　临走时，姑娘拿出水缸中的田
螺壳对谢端说："我走以后，你的日
子可能会有些艰苦，但只要你努力
干好农活，多打渔，多砍柴，生活会
一天一天好起来。我把田螺壳留给你，你可以用
它贮藏粮食，随你吃多少，壳里的稻米都不会吃完。"
　　两人正说话时，只见屋外狂风大作，大雨倾盆而下。姑娘说
完最后一句话后飘然离去。小伙子望着姑娘远去的方向，在雨
中伫立良久。

Before leaving, the fairy maiden picked up the shell and said to Xie Duan, "Your life may get a bit tougher after I leave. But as long as you work hard to do the farming, fishing and chopping, it will improve. I leave the empty shell to you and you can store your grain in it. It will never run out of rice. "

　At exactly this moment a fierce gale sprang up and the rain poured down outside. As she spoke her last words, the girl was swept out of the house and Xie Duan stood still in the rain watching her fade away.

　　为了感激神女的恩德，谢端特地为她造了一座神像，逢年过节都去烧香拜谢。姑娘留下的田螺壳能倒出许多米来，再加上他自己勤劳耕作，日子一天比一天红火起来。

　　几年之后，他娶了妻子，过上了美满幸福的日子。

　　To repay the fairy maiden's kindness, Xie Duan sculpted a special statue of her and burned incense to worship and thank her on every festival day. The shell of the river snail really did produce an abundance of rice, and Xie Duan himself kept working hard and prospered.

　　Several years later, he got married and led a happy life ever after.

完

End